New House For Mouse

WRITTEN BY
Fynisa Engler

ILLUSTRATED BY
Ryan Law

To my husband, Jeff, and my writing group:

Molly, Debi, and Jayne.—FE

This edition first published in 2022
by Lawley Publishing,
a division of Lawley Enterprises LLC

Hardcover ISBN 978-1-956357-83-7
Paperback ISBN 978-1-956357-85-1
Library of Congress Control Number: 2022936653

Lawley Publishing
70 S. Val Vista Dr. #A3 #188
Gilbert, AZ 85296
www.LawleyPublishing.com

LAWLEY
PUBLISHING

Mouse lay in bed and stared at the ceiling. He had arrived at Mama Bunny's foster home the night before. Mouse's mom couldn't take care of him right now, so he was staying with Mama Bunny and her other foster children.

"Mouse, breakfast," Mama Bunny called.

Mouse sighed. "I want to go home," he whispered.

At the kitchen table, Mouse's stomach growled as he rubbed his sleepy eyes. He sat staring at his breakfast.

"What's this?" Mouse asked, poking at the green leaves on his plate.

"Vegetables," said Mama Bunny.

"Don't you have pancakes?" Mouse asked.

"No, I'm sorry. Vegetables are Turtle's favorite. Plus, I want all my kiddos to grow up healthy and strong," said Mama Bunny.

Mouse was hungry, tired, and missed his mom.
"I don't like vegetables, and you're not my mom!" he
shouted as he ran to his room.

Mouse crawled under his bed. He thought about his mom.
He missed her so much and wanted to go home. He felt a
tear roll down his cheek. Just then, he heard a noise. A note
slid under his door.

To: Mouse

From: Hedgehog

Let's be friends.

Later, Mouse went to the kitchen for a snack. Hedgehog sat at the table drawing. As Mouse reached to open the fridge, he saw a list:

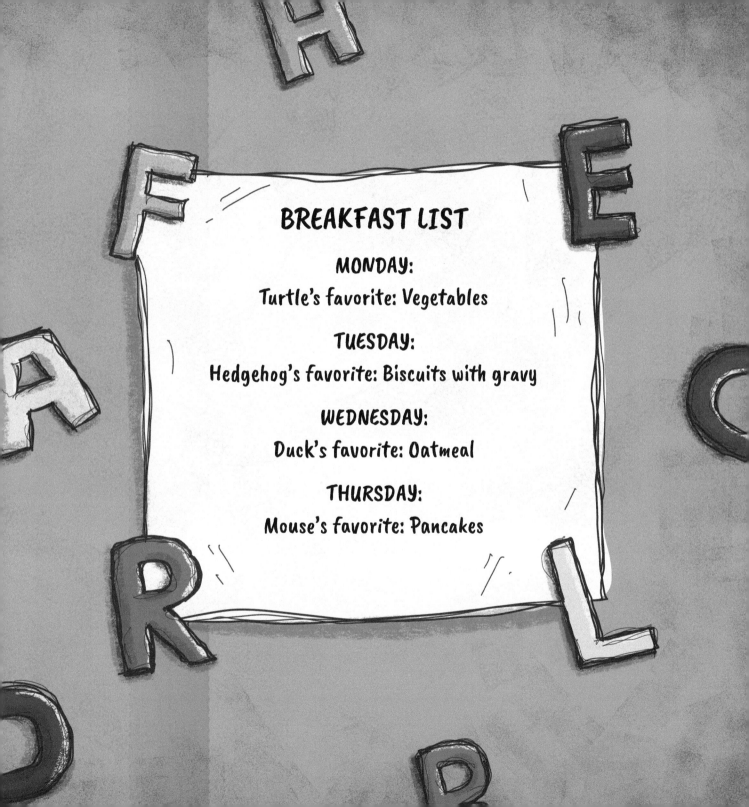

BREAKFAST LIST

MONDAY:
Turtle's favorite: Vegetables

TUESDAY:
Hedgehog's favorite: Biscuits with gravy

WEDNESDAY:
Duck's favorite: Oatmeal

THURSDAY:
Mouse's favorite: Pancakes

"Ohhh, pancakes, they're my favorite. My mom makes the best pancakes. I can't wait to go home," Mouse said.

"My mom makes the best biscuits and gravy," said Hedgehog. "Mama Bunny wants us to feel at home, so she makes our favorite foods."

Mouse sighed, "I still have three more days until it's my turn."

"You can have my spot tomorrow," Hedgehog offered.
"Really?" Mouse asked, surprised. "You sure?"
"Yep, that's what friends are for."

The next morning Mouse woke to the sweet smell of pancakes. He jumped out of bed and hurried to the kitchen.
Mouse frowned as he sat staring at his plate.

"Where are the chocolate chips?" he asked, confused.

"I'm sorry, I didn't know you wanted pancakes with chocolate chips," said Mama Bunny.

"It's okay," Mouse whispered, hanging his head. His mom always remembered to put chocolate chips in his pancakes. Mouse missed his mom more than ever and hoped to see her soon.

Hedgehog jumped from her chair and ran to the pantry. "We can sprinkle these on top," she said, holding a bag of chocolate chips.

Turtle and Duck cheered. Mouse's face brightened with a big smile.

The next morning, it was Duck's turn for his favorite breakfast.
"What's this?" Mouse asked, giving his bowl a shake.
"It's oatmeal. Try it. It's yummy," Hedgehog announced,
rubbing her tummy.
"It looks gross!" Mouse said as he scooped it and let it drip
from his spoon.

Hedgehog laughed, "It's because you didn't dress it up, silly."
Mouse then noticed the small bowls of bananas, strawberries, and apples.

"Mouse, we can't forget your favorite," Mama Bunny said, placing a bowl of chocolate chips on the table. He put some fruit and a handful of chocolate chips on top of his oatmeal.

Mouse took a small bite . . .
And another . . . and another.
"This IS yummy!" Mouse said
as he ate all of his oatmeal.

As the days passed, Mama Bunny's house began to feel more like home.

Hedgehog taught Mouse how to hold his nose when eating vegetables.

Mouse became the official pancake helper,
in charge of adding the chocolate chips.

He enjoyed cooking with Mama Bunny. Together, they tried new recipes to add to the breakfast list.

Mouse felt loved and part of a family.

He still missed his mom, and that was okay.

Fynisa Engler takes her love of writing children's books and combines it with her experiences in social work to create *New House For Mouse*. As a social worker, she has worked with many children just like Mouse. Fynisa aims for the reader to either personally relate to Mouse or develop understanding and empathy for those in foster care.

Fynisa lives in sunny Arizona with her husband, daughter, and three dogs named Belle, Lily, and Molly. She loves traveling and spending time with family and friends. She even enjoys Mondays because that's when she gets to work with her wonderful writing group.

Ryan Law loves animated movies/tv shows, video games, and soda pop. He is a kid at heart with a big imagination. He thinks stories written for kids are the best because they are allowed to be silly. He prefers drawing cartoons because they have no limits and can make you feel all the feels.

Want more insightful, empowering, fun children's books?
Want activities and links to go along with the story?
Visit us at www.lawleypublishing.com

For updates and info on New Releases follow us at

f lawleypublishing

@kidsbookswithheart

LAWLEY
PUBLISHING

Printed in the USA
CPSIA information can be obtained
at www.ICGtesting.com
LVHW070412131023
759262LV00045B/58